She chose a pretty dress to wear,

the prettiest she had.

For it was **Miffy's** birthday

and it showed that she was glad.

Happy Birthday, Miffy!

sang her mum and dad.

It's going to be lovely.

Miffy felt so glad.

You've made my chair so pretty,

with flowers, like on my dress.

How did you know I'd wear this one?

However did you guess?

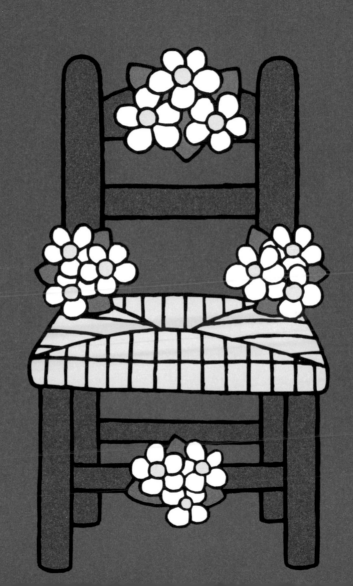

And what a stack of presents!

Are they all for me?

I'm feeling so excited,

let me open them and see.

Some scissors that can really cut,

a lovely whistle too.

And what I wanted, coloured pencils!

Miffy cheered, yahoo!

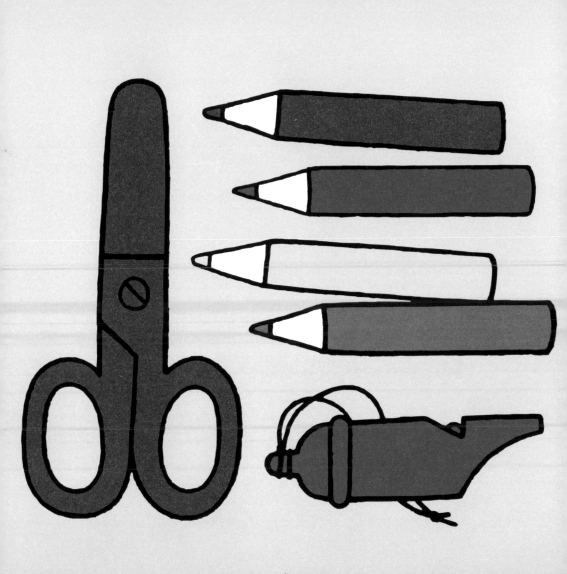

That afternoon her bunny friends,

Ag and Win, came by.

When they cried, Happy Birthday!

Miffy almost felt quite shy.

They took a ball out on the lawn

and didn't they have fun?

They played at lots and lots of games

until the day was done.

And in the evening Grandpa Bun

and Grandma came to tea

and they had brought a parcel too.

Whatever could it be?

A bear, a real woollen bear,

so sweet and soft, she said.

Tonight I really want to take him

up with me to bed.

They had a special dinner too,

with Grandpa on her right.

And Bear sat there on Miffy's lap,

which filled him with delight.

That night when Mummy Bun took Bear

and Miffy up to bed

– today was really wonderful,

thank you, Miffy said.

Original title: het feest van nijntje
Original text Dick Bruna © copyright Mercis Publishing bv, 1970
Illustrations Dick Bruna © copyright Mercis bv, 1970
This edition published in Great Britain in 2014 by Simon and Schuster UK Limited
1st Floor, 222 Gray's Inn Road, London WC1X 8HB, A CBS Company
Publication licensed by Mercis Publishing bv, Amsterdam
English re-translation by Tony Mitton © copyright 2014, based on the
original English translation of Patricia Crampton © copyright 1995
ISBN 978 1 4711 2076 3
Printed and bound by Sachsendruck Plauen GmbH, Germany
A CIP catalogue record for this book is available from the British Library upon request
10 9 8 7 6 5 4 3 2 1

www.simonandschuster.co.uk

MIX
From responsible
sources
FSC® C021195
www.fsc.org